Also by JOANN DAVIS

The Book of the Shepherd

HARPERONE
An Imprint of HarperCollins*Publishers*

The Well That Never Runs Dry

By the Scribe

As discovered by JOANN DAVIS

HarperOne

HarperCollins books may be purchased for educational, business, or sales promotional use. For information please write: Special Markets Department, HarperCollins Publishers, 10 East 53rd Street, New York, NY 10022.

HarperCollins website: http://www.harpercollins.com

HarperCollins®, 📖®, and HarperOne™ are trademarks of Harper-Collins Publishers

FIRST EDITION

Designed by Janet M. Evans

Library of Congress Cataloging-in-Publication Data
Davis, Joann.
    The well that never runs dry / by the Scribe, as discovered by Joann
Davis. — 1st ed.
        p. cm.
    ISBN 978–0–06–184468–3 1. Rare books—Fiction. I. Title.
PS3604.A9635W45 2011
813'.6—dc22   2010027063

11 12 13 14 15   RRD(H)   10 9 8 7 6 5 4 3 2 1

To the recklessly generous and
the relentlessly kind

To my mother,
Anna Loretta Margaret

Contents

Editor's Note to the Reader

LAST DECEMBER, WHEN I WENT TO THE POST OFFICE TO COLLECT my mail, there was a curious package waiting for me at the clerk's desk. Wrapped in crisp brown stationer's paper and lined with rows of exotic stamps, it bore the distinctive label of an antiquarian bookshop in Frankfurt, Germany, called Antiquariat Reinhold Streu.

To be honest, I felt like a small child at Christmas as I tore open the package, not knowing who had sent it or what was inside. The mystery deepened when a card tumbled out that was inscribed, "And will you do it again?"

Intrigued, I headed home to inspect my "Secret Santa" gift. It did not take a bibliophile to know that there was something quite special about the book it contained. Bound in vellum, it was impressed with the image of a woman holding a chalice in her outstretched hands as she stood on top of a rock. On the ground, by the woman's side, lay an unsheathed sword.

Drinking in the symbols, I felt like a thirsty traveler at a deep, rich well. But something else caught my eye. The size, look, and feel of this book were strikingly similar to *The Book of the Shepherd*. How did the mysterious sender know of my role in helping to get that earlier book translated and published? Were the two books related? I could only guess.

But it was not time for hypotheticals.

Opening the book, I perused the interior, hoping to find some exceptional marking or clue of origin. One thing was evident: like *The Book of the Shepherd*, this volume was written in an obscure language—a strange hybrid of Greek and Aramaic that I would later learn had not been spoken since the first century, or written since the late Renaissance. A team of linguists would be needed to decode it—perhaps the same group I had assembled for the Shepherd project.

And would I "do it again"?

Astute readers will ask: Is the manuscript that follows authentic? Should we put our faith in it? These are legitimate questions I plan to address in a separate publication. For now, let me state that I think truth, like beauty, is in the eye of the beholder. And let readers judge for themselves.

—JOANN DAVIS
Dorset, Vermont, February 2010

The Well That Never Runs Dry

The Best-Laid Plans

**HE DID NOT HEAR. SHE COULD NOT HEAR.**
She did not know. She could not know.
She did not help. She could not help.
Yet she suffered gravely for all that
she did not do to save the child's life.

It had happened on the morning of a day like all others.
Rising at dawn, she had packed her basket for a trip to the
river to wash her garments in the cool stream. She would go
quickly, work steadily, and be back before her family
awoke—that was her plan.

But on this morning, as she tiptoed past the bed where
her little girl lay sleeping, the child woke up.

"Look, Mama! Do you see me, Mama?" the girl called
out, waving her hands in the air. "I'll be your helper today."

Like a streak of lightning in a placid sky, the girl jumped
up and got dressed, slipping a crisp white tunic over her

head and sliding her feet into a tiny pair of sandals. She was four years old and proud of the help she gave her mother around the house, setting the table and filling the water pitcher. That she would soon be old enough to wear a sash and sit with the older girls at temple brought a smile to the girl's face, which was framed by an angelic halo of golden curls.

"Look, Mama!" she said as they began the short walk to the river. "I can shake like the belly dancer at the wedding feast." The tiny girl wiggled her reed-thin body and drummed her hand on an imaginary tambourine, hoping to brighten her mother's face.

But the woman was somber. She loved the girl with her whole heart and enjoyed tutoring her in the ways of women. But the possibility of lingering too long at the river and returning home too late to prepare breakfast for her ill-tempered husband struck fear in the woman's heart. She did not want to anger the man.

Motioning the girl to a sand pile near her washing place, the woman settled the child down to play. Then the woman began dipping her garments in the river, which was rough and rushing after a torrential rain. Each time the woman rinsed a sash or a tunic, she glanced over her shoulder and waved, making sure that the child was still busy with her make-believe games. All seemed well.

But the girl had tricks up her sleeve.

"Look, Mama!" the girl called out as she suddenly bolted up and ran toward the water. "I can jump like the temple dancers. . . ."

But as she skipped and gamboled toward the stream, she slipped on a mossy stone and slid down an embankment into the rushing water of the rain-swollen river. Sucked into a whirlpool, she was spun in vicious circles and then throttled like a rag doll.

"Mama!" she frantically called out as the swift current began to carry her downstream. "Mama!" she cried as she tried to stay afloat. But her mother was deaf and did not hear. And she did not know. And she did not come to help the child.

And later, when the girl's tiny body was found, the woman suffered gravely for all that she did not do to save the child's life.

In the Furnace of Affliction

HY DO THE RIGHTEOUS SUFFER?

Why does God take children before their time?

Why is the universe so cold, cruel, and unfair?

For centuries the people had asked these questions and for centuries the answers had come back the same from the elders and the prophets. The people suffer because the people sin. Suffering is punishment for the wrongs that are committed.

But was this true? Did a man reapeth as he soweth? Were evildoers bruised for their transgressions while the kind and the good were rewarded?

Elizabeth wondered. As she lay outstretched in an open field, beneath a blanket of twinkling stars, she thought about the day. It had begun at dawn on the outskirts of the village where she had gone to help deliver a baby. By all accounts the expectant mother was a good soul, a kind soul, who gave bread to every beggar at her table, and water to every supplicant at her well.

But as her labor progressed, the woman started to bleed profusely. Elizabeth did all that she could to stop the hemorrhaging, but the woman died, leaving behind a broken-hearted family whose loved one had been taken from them before her time.

Did the woman deserve to die? Where was divine justice when she needed it? Why had her acts of kindness not weighed in her favor on the scales of mercy? Why was a good life cut short?

Later the same day, Elizabeth had been asked to visit a child who had gotten the pestilence. The child was only one year old and not much bigger than a baby lamb. He had just begun to stand on his own two feet and toddle around, calling for his "ma-ma" and "pa-pa." So bright was his smile that hard hearts melted when they saw it.

But when the boy fell ill, his pain was so excruciating that it baffled the most learned apothecaries. The boy's pleading eyes begged for relief. But his mother was helpless.

When he died, Elizabeth placed small white stones on his eyelids to seal them for eternity.

Then at eventide, Elizabeth had been at the river, collecting herbs and spices for a meal she was preparing for her husband, Joshua, the shepherd. He was going to the High Ground to help resettle the villagers who had lost their dwellings in the flood. Elizabeth and her adopted brother, David, wanted to make a good meal for Joshua before he departed on his long, arduous walk with his sheep. Both were looking forward to spending time with the shepherd at the end of a long day.

But Elizabeth's plan took a sudden detour when she went to gather lilies along the edge of the river. She was in the brambles when she saw something out of the corner of her eye. What was this? Had someone left a garment behind? Perhaps a washerwoman or a slave had misplaced a scarf or sash belonging to a royal lady. If so, someone was in for a scolding. There would be hell to pay.

But as she went closer, Elizabeth was not so sure. Could a small child be playing hide-and-seek? The hour was late for this sort of game. But as Elizabeth inched forward she saw it—a small hand that looked like a starfish floating on the water. Amid the cattails and ornamental grass was the tiny body of a child, gently floating, facedown, her golden hair splayed across the water.

When she lifted the girl out of the marsh, Elizabeth brushed the hair back from the girl's face and dried it with her garment. The girl's lips were small and perfectly shaped, like the tiny petals of a miniature rose. If heaven was missing an angel, then Elizabeth had found her. She appeared to be in a very deep sleep. But it was the sleep of death, grim and final. Elizabeth held the child's tiny hand and then tidied her garment, readying her for the return to her family.

The task of telling the loved ones fell to Elizabeth, who led the mourners to the dwelling. It was pitch-black when the procession arrived. The house was dark, the mother waiting by the door, holding a candle, while her husband sat inside at a small wooden table in front of a large, uneaten plate of bread and fish. The distraught mother began to keen like a wounded animal when she saw the mourners carrying the stiff, tiny figure under the small white sheet.

Did the woman deserve this tragedy? Had she brought this misery down on herself? By what curse had she been marked?

As a man soweth, so shall he reapeth, the elders and the priests in the procession told her husband, who blamed his wife for failing to keep the child safe. And so he took a switch and beat her soundly for bringing shame and misfortune on his house.

A profound sadness washed over Elizabeth as she pondered these things. In her work as a midwife, she tried to bring light where it was dark, to spread joy where there was sorrow. But now the darkness was deep and abiding—it felt as if her light had gone out forever. How could she survive the furnace of affliction that was scorching her soul?

Her body shook as she called out to heaven, praying for answers. It was as she closed her eyes and began drifting off to sleep that she thought she heard a still, small voice whisper in her ear, *"Be still, little one, and know that I am."*

The Well That Never Runs Dry

LIZABETH SLEPT. SHE DREAMED THAT SHE was in a faraway place with green pastures and rolling hills. At the crossroads of this mysterious place was an Old Woman with long silver hair, who was sitting on top of a trunk.

"Hello," said the Old Woman. "Are you looking for something?"

"How do you know?" Elizabeth asked.

"By that look on your face. Most people who come here are trying to find the Well That Never Runs Dry. I can point you to it. But first you'll need to do some soul-searching."

Elizabeth watched as the Old Woman cleansed her hands with a special cloth she kept in her trunk. Then she reached inside Elizabeth's body and drew out an orb.

"Don't worry," the Old Woman said, putting the orb into Elizabeth's hands. "It's indestructible, so nothing bad can happen to it."

Elizabeth knelt down to examine the orb, which was small, like a fortune-teller's ball. On the outside, it was quite ordinary.

But as she peered inside, Elizabeth saw what she could never have imagined. A cluster of light particles at the center of the orb was glowing gloriously, like ethereal embers in a heavenly hearth. The particles pulsated when Elizabeth smiled.

"Hmm," the Old Woman said, pointing to some particles that seemed to have lost their luster. "Have you been upset and discouraged lately?"

"Does it matter?" Elizabeth asked.

"Very much," said the Old Woman. "Your soul is a lamp that burns best with the Oil of Serenity in its well. Despair dims the light."

Elizabeth thanked the Old Woman for her observations. But this oil—where could it be found? It was not sold in the market with the figs and dates. It was not pressed with the olives that grew in her grove.

"Each morning," the Old Woman offered, "before you rise from your bed, imagine the sun streaming into you, filling your lamp with serenity, making you whole. Let the light pour into you each day."

"And if I do?" Elizabeth asked as the Old Woman put her soul back in place.

But that was it. The dream was done.

Beginning the Journey

THE NEXT MORNING, UPON SEEING THE sun come up, Elizabeth lay still and let the light pour into her lamp, filling it with the Oil of Serenity, making her whole. Then she rose to her feet and began her day.

Waking David, she made breakfast for her brother and told him they were going on a journey to find the Well That Never Runs Dry. "I have dreamed of it," Elizabeth told the boy, explaining that they would travel while Joshua was away.

But first they would visit the deaf woman whose child had died, to see how she was doing.

After fetching donkeys and packing provisions, they began to walk. The sun was high and the air was hot as they made their way to the little dwelling where Elizabeth had gone the night before. Leading the mourners, she had returned the child to her mother, then stood graveside in the moonlight, as the girl was buried at midnight.

Now, in the bright light of morning, Elizabeth hoped to see the mother again. To hold her hand and dry her tears. To sow seeds of solace in a field of despair.

But when she approached the house, the place looked deserted, its windows shuttered, its front door nailed shut.

"Hello," Elizabeth called out as she and David circled the garden. The long dark shadows of the midday sun had cast a pall over the flowers, crisscrossing them with black lines and ominous *x*'s.

"Hello," Elizabeth called out again. But the place was quiet.

Baffled, Elizabeth took David's hand and headed to the meadow. Perhaps the mother was there, standing sentinel at the tear-stained, stone-lined place where her child was buried, rooted to the spot by the tendrils of love.

But when she and David approached the grave, it was quiet, not a creature stirring. Kneeling, they prayed, picked flowers, and were preparing to leave when they saw an old woman leaning up against a tree. Still as a stone, she wore a light blue garment tied at the waist with a bright green sash.

A long braid of silver hair hung over her shoulder and down to her waist.

"Cousin," Elizabeth said, recognizing that the woman was Miriam, the old seamstress from the town beyond the hill. "What brings you here?"

"News from the potter who heard from the baker that a child has died," the old woman said. "I walked all night to comfort the mother whose broken heart still beats."

"The mother—" Elizabeth asked expectantly. "Is she here?"

"Not since dawn," the old woman said, her voice trailing off. She cast her eyes to the ground and, like a stubborn mule, refused to go on.

"Cousin," Elizabeth prompted gently. "What do you know?"

"That the priests in their high hats and embroidered coats came at dawn, quoting Old Law on wives, women, and obedience," Miriam said. "They cut her hair and ordered the husband to cast her out."

"The husband—" Elizabeth asked. "Why did he not resist?"

"At first he defied them, saying, 'You have no power here. She loved the child. Be gone.' But when they threatened to burn his crops and blacken his name, he beat her and turned her over to them. Now she is gone to an unknown place, with sorrow as her companion."

Overcome by sadness, Elizabeth prayed for some Oil of Serenity to fill her lamp. She asked heaven to bathe her in light and rid her soul of despair. Then she turned to Miriam, whose feet were red and swollen.

"Cousin," she said, "you have walked a long way on rough roads. Let us refresh you."

The old woman smiled as David kneeled down to loosen her sandals. The boy got balm from the side saddle on his donkey and rubbed oil and perfume into the old seamstress's feet. Then Elizabeth set out a simple repast of fruits and nuts for everyone to enjoy.

When all had eaten their fill, Miriam braided the tails of David's and Elizabeth's donkeys and decorated their manes with daisies. The animals clip-clopped around in a joyous circle as Elizabeth and David looked on, smiling.

"Boy," Miriam said to David, "you sate my hunger and quench my thirst. You soothe my feet and uplift my spirit. How am I to repay you?"

The youngster smiled and drew close to the old woman, attracted like a little bee to a sweet cache of nectar. Miriam stroked his dark head of hair affectionately. Then the old woman turned to Elizabeth and took her hand.

"You are packed for a long walk," Miriam said. "Where are you going?"

"To find the Well That Never Runs Dry," Elizabeth said. "I have dreamed of it. We will journey while Joshua is gone to the High Ground to resettle the flood victims."

"The well," Miriam said. "Grandmother spoke of it when she lay dying. She wanted to go in search of it herself, but she was too crippled and old to make the journey. Instead she gave me a tapestry embroidered with symbols that shows the way."

Elizabeth's eyes widened as she listened. "This tapestry—where is it now?" the young woman asked.

"I keep it hidden in the stone pocket of my hearth," Miriam said.

"Why such care?" Elizabeth asked.

"The well's water is potent," Miriam said. "And the potent fear it. For whosoever shall drink of the water shall have new life."

Thoughts raced through Elizabeth's head like a rushing river after an intense rain. She reached out to Miriam and held her hand.

"Cousin," Elizabeth said. "This tapestry may uncover riches long buried." The young woman paused, hoping her cousin would understand what words could not express.

"Yes," said Miriam, looking into Elizabeth's blue eyes and finding a sea of goodness and faith there. "My spirit tells me so." The old seamstress fell quiet. But a question burning inside her could not be suppressed.

"Cousin," Miriam said to her companions. "I am crooked and slow and sometimes my feet get sore. But my spirit is strong and my heart is willing. May I join you on your journey?"

A Trio of Travelers

ND SO IT WAS THAT THEY BEGAN THEIR walk guided by the tapestry retrieved from the stone pocket of Miriam's hearth. They traveled over hill and dale. They walked on stone paths and in green meadows. And at the end of their first day they came to a village square where they met the Storyteller.

He was seated in his usual spot, inside his tent, surrounded by pillows, old parchments, jars of ink, and an assortment of foods. Wearing a bright red turban on his head and a gold sash around the waist of his white tunic, he was a colorful sight. Seeing them approach, he put down his stylus and scroll, waved his hands in the air, and issued a hearty greeting.

"Come in. Sit down. Join me for a meal!" he said. "My table is rich. There is food enough for all."

Spread out on the ground before him, on a golden square of silk, were fruits, nuts, salted fish, olives, honey, and other delights. Looking at the rich assortment made David's mouth water. The boy had walked a good distance on an empty stomach and was famished. But he tried his best to be polite, as the shepherd and Elizabeth had taught him to be.

"Our stomachs are empty but so, too, are our coin purses," the boy said. As he spoke, the smell of the food pricked his nostrils and his mouth watered even more in anticipation of a savory meal. David looked to Elizabeth, hoping she would strike a bargain with this kind and friendly man.

"Perhaps a story will please you," Elizabeth offered. "We have many tales to tell."

"I make my living telling them," the Storyteller responded. "I never tire of hearing them."

So they all ate and drank. And they told their tales.

ᖡ MIRIAM'S TALE ᖡ

THERE ONCE WAS A GIRL WHO LIVED ON A FARM WHERE MANY animals were born. The girl loved animals—especially the tiniest babies—and often curled up to sleep with them at night. The newborn calves and lambs had warm, chubby bellies and little pink tongues that were sticky and scratchy when they licked the girl's cheek. She could sit for hours petting the babies and watching them suckle. In the barn, tending animals, the girl knew endless joy.

"You love baby animals," a herdsman said. "When you are grown, why not become a shepherdess? Then you will be with the animals all day. At night you will share their warmth and never be alone. A shepherdess is a friend to all animals and you are that!"

The little girl went to sleep that night thinking of what it would be like to spend her life on the hill all day, in the sun, tending the animals. This could be a good life, she thought, full of caring and love and fine, fresh air.

But the next day, she was in the kitchen cutting potatoes with a sharp knife, preparing vegetables for a great vat of soup.

"You have a knack for slicing quickly and evenly," her old auntie said. "The meals you prepare are delicious, their aromas alluring. Why not become a cook and spend your days by the hearth? The farmhands will appreciate your thick stews. The children will yelp for your creamy porridges. And many will think fondly of you when their bellies are full."

The girl went to bed and dreamed of being a cook, working all day by the hearth, making soup and bread. In her dreams she could smell the fresh bread toasting and her mouth watered. A life as a cook would allow her to live in the company of women, who were nurturing and kind.

But the next day, the girl was with her old grandmother in her garden. "Little one," the very old woman said. "You tend the seedlings well. Why not become a gardener as I did when I was a young maiden? Be the one who plants the crops and brings the food to table. Even the King honors the harvesters with their own festival. What do you say?"

The girl was quiet. She loved her grandmother with her whole heart and did not want to disappoint the old woman whose council had always been rich and rewarding. The wisdom of such an elder was rare and hard to find. The girl fell silent, pondering all the recommendations she had received.

Be a shepherdess.

Be a cook.

Be a gardener.

Each who had offered a suggestion had her best interest at heart.

Yet, inside her, a still, small voice was whispering. It spoke of a purpose yet unknown. A purpose she needed to look within to find.

The next morning, the girl went to the hill and sat quietly. She took her needle and thread and began to make a neat row of stitches. Time passed, but she did not notice the many hours that flew by. As she wove the thread into the cloth, as her fingers danced over the fabric, fabulous patterns became visible. A picture was coming to life. She felt calm and reassured. And so she continued.

And as she sewed, she listened to the voice inside that was always there, helping her know what was right and wrong. This voice was gentle and kind and never led her astray if she took time to listen to it.

And so it was after several minutes that she looked to the sky and spoke to heaven.

"Dear God," she said. "When I grow up, I want to be myself."

From that day on, Miriam said, the girl took a needle and thread and sat on the hill every time she needed to think. When she sat and stitched, she was close to God and herself and her own heart. Soon, her fingers became expert, though no one had ever taught her to sew. They moved swiftly over the cloth, creating even stitches in neat rows. And soon she had sewn a great and luxurious garment that was fit for a king.

One day the King announced a contest inviting every seamstress in the land to prepare a garment for his daughter to wear at her wedding. The budding seamstress labored in secret, ascending to the hilltop at night to work by the light of the moon. In no time she had produced the most beautiful gown. But she was shy and unwilling to enter the competition.

Hearing rumors of the reluctant seamstress, the King insisted on meeting the girl whose skills were extolled by the women in his wife's retinue. She came to the palace and showed her creation.

Soon she was being celebrated as a most capable seamstress. Her talents long hidden to most became known to all. Children who wanted to learn to sew came from miles around. And she taught them.

And she sat in a circle with women who liked to stitch and mend, tack and hem, lengthen and shorten. Together they made tattered garments whole, cut new patterns, and even designed tapestries for the royal halls. And, while she sewed, the women talked and listened. Though she worked with her hands, she was guided by her heart. And many wore her clothes on their backs.

"I know," said Miriam. "I was that girl. And now I make my living as a seamstress. I cut new forms. I repair old garments. And when I sew I listen to what can be heard only in the stillness of my soul. My heart beats a rhythm of its own. And I hear the words not spoken."

"Ah," said the Storyteller. "Thank you for telling your tale. Now I know you. A woman of purpose."

Elizabeth spoke next, grateful for the chance to repay her host.

THE UNDESERVING ONE

ONCE THERE WAS A SERVANT GIRL WHO LIVED IN THE ROYAL palace. Though she had been born into servitude and never tasted freedom, the girl was happy. She loved rising early to pick vegetables and flowers. She liked dancing on feast days and plaiting the hair of the royal ladies. Most of all, she loved everyone in the servants' quarters, with whom she shared a spirit of camaraderie.

But one day, trouble began brewing. A new girl had come to live at the palace and, like a tight pair of sandals, she rubbed the other girls the wrong way.

"She is lazy," said one of the young servants. "She sleeps late while others sweat and toil. We rise early to fetch water from the well but she dallies in her bed."

"She is haughty," said another girl. "She breaks bread in her room, by herself, not at table with the rest. When others are hungry, she denies them a piece of her crust."

"And she is vain," still another girl chimed in. "When we dip and pound our garments at the river, she marvels at her own reflection in the pool, saying, 'Am I not as beautiful as the lady of the house?'"

Over time, bad stories about the new girl became as numerous and as prickly as the stinging nettles in a briar patch. She was vilified and ignored. When she needed help, few came to her aid. Those who did were scoffed at and ridiculed.

"Fool!" someone said to the happy servant girl, when they saw her helping the new girl gather up her laundry from the rocks on the riverbanks before the storm clouds burst. "She does nothing for you. Why be kind and good to the undeserving one?"

The happy servant girl had no answer. Instead, she covered her ears, trying to ignore the angry wagging tongues.

But a sadness grew inside her. One day, after seeing the new girl shunned once more, the happy servant girl went to see the Midwife, the oldest and wisest woman in the royal house. The Midwife used her large, elegant hands to catch babies and nurture new mothers. Over many years she had delivered hundreds of children of the poor and the rich, of the beautiful and the awkward, without judgment, never discriminating.

"What brings you here?" the Midwife asked the once happy young servant who appeared sad one night on her doorstep.

"A new girl has come to live in our midst and the wagging tongues say that she is vain, selfish, and lazy," the once happy girl said. "But when the lady scolds her, she too needs a cloth to dry her tears. Shall I not love the undeserving one?"

The Midwife needed no time to think.

"Child," she said, stroking her cheek. "What is love? Is it a reward bestowed on the deserving? Must it be earned?

"But as a great teacher once said, 'If you love those who love you, what credit is that to you? For even sinners love those who love them. And if you do good to those who do good to you, what credit is that to you? For even sinners do the same.

"'And if you lend to those from whom you hope to receive, what credit is that to you? For even sinners lend to sinners, to receive as much again.

"'For I say to you that love is not a favor or a reward bestowed on the good. Love is its own reward. And if you give love, expect nothing in return. And if you love your enemies and are kind to the ungrateful and turn your cheek to those who have insulted you, then surely you have lived the Higher Law.'"

The girl looked into the old woman's eyes and there she found a sea of kindness.

"I know," said Elizabeth. "I was that girl. And that day I was reminded to touch not the blade of the cynic or the judge, for that blade cuts, but rather to try always to drink from the chalice of love."

"Thank you," said the Storyteller. "Now I know you. A person who knows the true meaning of love."

David spoke next, grateful for a chance to repay his generous host with a story.

💧 DAVID'S STORY 💧

ONCE THERE WAS A BOY WHO WAS FULL OF WOE.

"Woe is me!" he said. "Woe is me! Why must I suffer so? Why am I the victim of such misfortune?"

If the boy got a thorn in his foot, he cursed the bush.

If the boy got a speck in his eye, he cursed the wind.

If the boy heard a bad word from his father, he sulked all day and night.

"I am cursed," he said. "Nothing is ever right. Why me?" he asked. "Why me?"

One day, the boy was on the hill with a shepherd. The storm clouds on the horizon were dark and forbidding. They threatened to bring a ferocious rain that frightened the boy.

"Be quick!!" the boy shouted. "A storm is gathering. Take cover. Gather the sheep."

But the shepherd did not panic. Smiling, he stood fast and let the last rays of sun enter his soul, filling him with serenity, making him whole.

The boy was perplexed. He could not understand why the shepherd was not moving quickly. A storm was gathering. Yet the shepherd was calm.

"Why are you smiling?" asked the boy.

"Because the land is dry and needs water," the shepherd said. "Because the animals are thirsty and need to drink. Because the buds are sprouting and the water will help them blossom. Because I like to swim in the river and it is low."

The boy was quiet. He listened.

"Though the storm clouds may come and force me to take cover," the shepherd said, "I look for the silver lining."

The boy listened. A few seconds passed. And the shepherd continued.

"You wish to be a scribe, do you not? For you have told me so," the shepherd said. "But can the scribe's papyrus grow where there is no marsh? Can reed flourish where there is no water?"

Turning inward, the boy looked at the gloom and pessimism in his soul and wondered who had planted it there. He yearned to replace the bitter with the sweet. To look not through a glass darkly but to see in full. That day the boy began to see through new eyes.

"I know," said David. "I was that boy. Now, when the storm comes, I ask not why is this happening *to* me, but rather why is this happening *for* me."

"Ah," said the Storyteller. "Thank you for telling your tale. Now I know you. David, the boy who looks to find a blessing in disguise."

The Storyteller's Tale

HEIR STORIES TOLD, THE THREE TRAVELERS
watched the late afternoon sun begin to
die. It was time to bed down the donkeys
and retire to a nearby inn. But as they
got ready to depart, Elizabeth turned to
the Storyteller.

"And you, friend. Before we get on our way, would you
honor us with a tale?"

Instead of answering, the Storyteller kneeled down on
the ground and began digging until he came upon a slate
gray rock. He set the rock to the side, then burrowed some
more, until he came upon some pink pebbles and brown
stones. In no time, he had a small pile of stones in front of
him. Turning to his guests he asked, "Do you know the
story of the Rock Collector?"

❧ THE ROCK COLLECTOR ❧

THERE ONCE WAS A MAN WHO LOVED ROCKS AND COLLECTED them from the time he was a small boy. Big rocks and little rocks, pebbles and large stones, flat rocks, round rocks, rocks of every shape and color—grays, pinks, earthen reds, and deep browns. He gathered them all and mixed them together in a great mountain of stone.

Over time, the boy grew up and so did the mountain. It became so big that it dwarfed his house. When the boy became a man and married, the mountain embarrassed his wife, who wondered what purpose there was in this enormous stone pile.

"Your rocks have made us the laughingstock of our neighbors," she remarked. "And for what? What good can come of them?"

This was not the first time the man had encountered doubt and criticism. But he did not mind. He loved his rocks and enjoyed experimenting with them. He made walls that held back the flood tide when the river surged after a terrible rain. He put his rocks into the fire and found that they held heat that could be used to warm the bed of his sick mother when she trembled with the chills. He used his rocks to make a circle of stones at camp to ring in the fire. A good man, of good intentions, he studied his rocks to see how he might put them to noble use.

One day, while sitting at the campfire, the man saw some of the rocks soften and a molten stream of ore began to bleed out of them. Soft and pliable, the ore could be scooped up and fashioned into many shapes that later hardened.

Very interesting, thought the man, entranced by the discovery. *What shall I do with this?*

Enlisting the help of his wife, the man gathered the soft ore and began molding it. First, the man made buckets to carry water, then long spoons to stir hot pots and little spoons to use at table. Eventually he made bracelets and earrings to adorn his wife's body. She was a handsome woman and he used his skills to complement her beauty.

Eventually he made an extraordinary chalice that could be used to sip the finest wines. The priests and royalty liked the chalice so much that they commissioned the man to make other grails for use in the most sacred ceremonies. He accepted the commission with heartfelt gratitude.

The man soon had a new livelihood of making beautiful objects that enhanced life. His creativity enriched the world. People came from miles around to see his handicrafts.

One day, when the man was working with ore, he molded a loop big enough to put his foot through. This gave him more stability when he sat upon his horse—more stability than the toe loop made of rope that kept most horsemen in place. He worked on this foot holder, molding the metal. He hoped that with greater stability he could ride faster in delivering hot stones to warm the beds of sick villagers.

"What are you doing?" his wife asked when she saw him making his foot loop.

"Give me a name," the man said. "I have created something new and I need to christen it."

"What is it?" asked the wife.

"A loop for my foot. A loop that allows me to anchor myself and ride steadily on my horse, so that I can maneuver the animal and even stand up while I am riding, holding the reins with only one hand."

Soon the man was turning out "stirrups," a new invention that people from miles around heard about and came to inspect. The stirrups gave every rider standing tall in the saddle a chance to steer the horse with greater ease. Using stirrups, the inventor could ride swiftly to deliver hot stones to the sick, with new, assured control.

News of the stirrup quickly reached the King, an ambitious man who owned vast tracts of land but was never satisfied with his holdings.

"Bring this Rock Collector to me," the King said. A messenger went to summon the man and he came.

"Your stirrups please me," the King said. "Now, instead of riding in low, slow chariots, with one hand fixed on the reins, my men can stand and fight from the high perch of swift-moving horses, controlling the animals with their feet while wielding swords, knives, and lances."

The Rock Collector squinted and squirmed as he listened. He had never thought of using the foot holder for war. But the King was quite certain that a stirrup would give him great power and dominion over others. His will for destruction was vast. He glorified the sword and entreated his militia to do the same. His black heart was on a perverse mission to subordinate.

Soon the King opened a foundry to make stirrups from ore extracted from rocks gathered from miles around. Impatient and intolerant, the King forced his subjects to toil like worker ants in the deadly heat of the sun. Hundreds of pairs of stirrups were forged each day, and for a long while, the King was the only man with an army of horsemen riding swiftly and hurling spears. He quickly conquered the surrounding populations.

Women and children were killed. Old people scattered when they saw the horsemen coming. The horse and the rider seemed to be one as they moved quickly, the rider poised to strike like deadly lightning.

The Rock Collector and his wife were baffled. They could not understand how tiny pebbles brought massive plundering. How the ore that had given rise to the chalice had also formed the blade, the sword, and the spear. How the peaceful imagination that forged the chalice had led to such creative destruction.

Terrified, the man went in search of large rocks that could serve as tablets. On these tablets, with a sharp chisel, he set down "The Tale of the Chalice and the Stirrup" and he asked his family to memorize the tale and tell the tale far and wide in case the tablets were chipped, shattered, or lost over time. The tale was shared with scribes who created parchment copies that were sent out into the world to be read by storytellers.

"I know," said the Storyteller, "because I have memorized the tale and tell it as often as I can. For now I know that creativity is a means to an end. But which will it be? Will we construct or destroy? Each one of us chooses by the power of our intention."

When he had finished his tale, the Storyteller turned to Elizabeth. "You are packed for a long journey," he said. "Where are you going?"

"To find the Well That Never Runs Dry," Elizabeth said. "I have dreamed of it."

"Many have gone looking for it," the Storyteller said. "But none has found it. Perhaps they did not go deep enough to find the source."

"Storyteller," Elizabeth said. "You speak in riddles. What do you know?"

"You shall discover it soon enough," the Storyteller said, "when partners join hands and the gentle time comes."

And with that, the Storyteller closed his book on the day.

The Initiation

HE MYSTICAL GLOW OF DUSK HAD DESCENDED on the land. Nobody liked this time of day better than Elizabeth did.

After settling Miriam down at the inn and helping David tend the donkeys, Elizabeth walked to the top of a nearby hill and watched the hot, orange sun dip below the horizon. It was a magnificent sight that filled her soul with awe and wonder. She thought of the shepherd and promised the dusk that she would keep her heart as light as a feather.

But as the light began to fade, Elizabeth felt sad. She was lonely. She missed Joshua.

The shepherd had been gone now for two days, his longest separation from Elizabeth since the two had gotten married a few years earlier. They had met through David, who worked in the market until one fateful morning when the boy had overslept and arrived late to the fruit and vegetable stall. The shepherd had been nearby that day, watering his sheep, when he heard a small boy crying and rushed forward to find David on the ground, in the dirt, beneath his angry father's switch. The shepherd had tended the boy's wounds before going his own way.

But the drama was not done.

The next day, when the shepherd went to check on the boy, he discovered that David had been disowned by his father and adopted by Elizabeth, a former slave. The young woman invited the shepherd to partake of a rich meal in the cool shade of her garden. Together they ate fish, drank wine, played music, and danced. Then Elizabeth asked the shepherd if she and David could join him on his journey of discovery to find the mysterious "new way" that had been revealed in his dream. The shepherd hoped that the "new way" would create a more peaceful world. He was heartened to discover that Elizabeth had a map, given to her by her grandfather, that seemed connected to the mystery.

Soon, they were traveling to a cave near the Great Inland Sea where they uncovered a jug containing a scroll inscribed with the Law of Substitution. It said:

Make me a channel of your peace
Where there is hatred, let me sow love
Where there is injury, let me sow pardon
Where there is doubt, let me sow faith
Where there is despair, let me sow hope
Where there is sadness, let me sow joy
Where there is darkness, let me bring light
For it is in giving that we receive
It is in pardoning that we are pardoned
And it is in dying that we are born to eternal life
For this is the Law of Substitution.

The Law had become their credo. Upon returning home from the Great Inland Sea, they devoted themselves to living and working as instruments of peace. Joshua opened a healing sanctuary for sick animals. David studied with the local scribe to be able to record life-affirming stories. As for Elizabeth, she found a bold new path to walk—or perhaps it found her.

It happened one evening, shortly after she, Joshua, and David had moved into the old house left to Elizabeth by her grandfather. The hour was late. Joshua and David were already asleep, and Elizabeth was preparing for bed when a knock at the door pierced the still night.

Wrapping herself in a shawl, Elizabeth went to answer, not sure who could be calling at such a late hour. Lost animals sometimes wandered from the rocky road into the shepherd's verdant meadow for a nibble of his tall green grass. Sometimes a herder on a rescue mission came to retrieve a stray calf or lamb.

But what Elizabeth found on her threshold could not have been imagined. In front of her was a little girl wearing a bright red head scarf and holding a glowing torch in her outstretched hand.

"Please, woman," the small girl said in a thin, pleading voice. "My sister suffers. Come quick!"

Waking Joshua, Elizabeth took the girl's hand and rushed to the far side of the road where a young woman no more than twenty years old lay outstretched beneath a blanket on a flatbed wagon. The young woman's knees were drawn up to her chest. She was biting her lip. And her face wore a mask of pain.

"Please," the young woman pleaded through gritted teeth. "Can you lift this bitter cup from me?"

Instinctively, Elizabeth knew that the young woman was not sick. She was in labor. What she needed were skilled hands—healing hands—to guide her through childbirth and catch her baby.

But was there time to fetch the Midwife, who lived over the mountain? The hour was late, the roads dark, and the journey arduous. The Midwife was old and feeble, unable to travel as quickly and easily as she did in her prime.

"Please," the young woman called out again, anxiously. "Deliver me from this trial!"

It was then and there that Elizabeth knew—this was her initiation. Her time. She was being called to serve.

Rolling up her sleeves, she asked Joshua to bring water and clean cloth. Sleepy-eyed David was plucked from his bed to care for the little girl—to give her milk and bread and to distract her from the commotion. He rose quickly and did as needed.

And then Elizabeth set to work, doing simple things that she had seen the royal midwife do.

She held the young woman's hand to comfort her.

She stroked the young woman's cheek to calm her.

She mopped the young woman's brow to cool her.

She wet the young woman's parched lips to slake her thirst.

She rallied the woman from the abyss of tiredness into which she was sinking. Using soft words and gentle murmurings, she implored the woman to dig deep inside herself to bring forth what was within her—her courage, strength, and endurance. For if she could bring forth what was within her, she could withstand most any trial.

This Elizabeth believed, and she stood ready to help.

Hours passed. The night wore on, and the trial was long and arduous. There seemed to be no end in sight. But then, suddenly, Elizabeth knew the final stage of the woman's trial had come.

"Push!" she urged the woman, taking her hand. "Bear down." And together they worked, like one soul in two bodies, their two hearts beating as one. They were kindred spirits in a life-affirming partnership.

When the moon was at the highest point in its arc, the sound of a baby wailing broke the silent night. Elizabeth pulled the baby from its mother's loins, as she had often seen Joshua do in birthing a lamb. She laid the baby at its mother's breast to suckle and watched them fall asleep, the baby's face smooth and calm, the mother's face wrinkled and exhausted. A moment of peace descended. An epic struggle was over.

Word soon spread of the moonlight birth. Of the impatient baby born on the back of a wagon. Of the baby who did not wait for the Midwife but who was brought into the world by Elizabeth, who sang a welcome song and swaddled the newborn in a soft cotton cloth.

Shortly after, Elizabeth apprenticed herself to the Midwife beyond the hills, who wished to retire after long years of difficult work. Elizabeth was soon known to all as "the Gentle Midwife." Whenever a child was due to be born, the villagers called upon Elizabeth. Within a very short time, she was a part of every household, a member of every family, sharing happy times and tears, easy births and grave trials.

There were the twins that came miraculously, bringing double joy. And there were tragic, calamitous stillbirths. And infants who were born blind. And children who died young. Always at Elizabeth's side was Joshua, her companion and friend, who helped whenever she needed an extra set of hands, a gentle presence, and a soft voice. Elizabeth had come to need, rely, and depend on him.

But now he was gone, off resettling the victims of the flood. Elizabeth missed him. Like sun on soil, he warmed her. Like branch to blossom, he lifted her. Like a life raft in a raging storm, he raised her up with love, helping her know that love is the answer. That love is the way. That only love is right and real.

Looking out on the horizon, Elizabeth watched the sun disappear and be replaced by a canopy of stars. She was tired after a long day.

And so she went back to the inn, made her way up to the room where Miriam slept, next door to David, and was soon fast asleep.

A New Day

HEY ROSE EARLY, CONSULTED THE TAPESTRY, and were leaving the village when they heard it—

Plink. Plunk. Plink. Plunk.

Again and again, the noise resounded—

Plink. Plunk. Plink. Plunk.

David sprang forward, tracking the sound to the edge of the village where the Lamplighter lived. Old and frail, with a long white beard that hung down to his waist, he was in his grove, eating olives.

Plink. Plunk. Plink. Plunk.

His olive pits landed in an earthen jug.

"Welcome," the Lamplighter said, looking up. He was not expecting visitors so early in the day. Dusk was when most patrons came for candles and oil.

But here they were—three morning guests. Standing still, in the sun, they waited as the Lamplighter finished his breakfast and swung open his gate. "You look famished," he told the travelers. "Come in."

Grateful, David skipped inside the grove to comb the vines.

But Elizabeth and Miriam held back. An old tapestry full of esoteric symbols on a table near the gate caught their eye.

"Old man," Miriam said, stroking the fabric. "This cloth is mysterious. What tale does it tell?"

"Of the Well That Never Runs Dry," the Lamplighter said. "Many have gone looking for it but none has returned. Perhaps they got lost in the Sun Maze at the Great Stone Quarry. It's a dangerous place near the Sacred Lake."

Elizabeth's eyes widened. She was bursting with questions. But David jumped in first.

"Old man," the boy said, licking his lips. "The fruits of your grove delight me. But what of the fruits of your labor?" David pointed to the Lamplighter's small white hut by the side of the road. Shrouded in shade, this mysterious place beckoned him.

Smiling, the Lamplighter took David's hand and led the way into a small room crowded with grinding stones, beeswax, wicks, ingots, vessels, vials, and stray lantern parts. Here in this workshop, the Lamplighter made candles, repaired lamps, and pressed oil.

"Boy," the illuminator said, peering into David's bright blue eyes. "Can you see in the dark?"

David remained quiet, knowing that some questions were like unripe fruit on the vine—best left dangling.

"But if a child becomes sick at night," the Lamplighter continued, "how will you make your way to the High Ground to fetch the physician?"

The question made David think of the shepherd, who had been gone for a few days now. Suddenly the boy's heart ached. He yearned to walk and talk with his friend, who had taught him many things. What would the shepherd say in answer to the Lamplighter's question? The boy searched inside himself for the right response.

"Old man," the boy said, after a short while. "The owl sees in the dark. So, too, the bat and the possum. Even the lowly snake, whose belly scrapes the ground, moves smoothly at night, navigating the slippery rocks. But a boy needs a lamp to guide his feet or he may stumble and fall. My friend Joshua, the shepherd, who is off on the High Ground, tells me so."

"Ah," said the Lamplighter, his eyes glistening. "Your friend Joshua is wise. But if Joshua's lamp goes out, what then?" As he spoke, the Lamplighter snuffed out a candle still burning from the night before. Its thin funnel of smoke curled up into the air and hung there, obscuring the boy's sight, until the Lamplighter blew it away.

"Joshua packs his pouch with what he needs," David said proudly. "Spare wicks and oil go with us on every journey."

"And if his supplies run out?" the Lamplighter asked.

"The market is never far," Elizabeth joined in. She and Miriam had followed the boy into the hut and now they were at his side, offering encouragement.

"Yes," Miriam added. "Joshua knows the source of good and plenty."

"I see," the Lamplighter said, stroking his long beard. "It is not enough to light the fire. You must tend the flame—feed it." Turning to his hearth, the Lamplighter stoked the dying embers. Soon flames were shooting up and the Lamplighter's careworn face was bathed in light.

But David, distracted, had moved on to look at a cabinet in a distant corner of the Lamplighter's workshop.

"What's this?" David said, poking his nose into a large black cauldron full of brown and green olive pits. The boy scooped some up in his hands, then let them rain back down, like drops in a summer shower.

"Many value the fruit's flesh and oil," the Lamplighter said. "But I boil and grind the pit, looking for what is at the center. The *essence*."

Elizabeth stared at the man. Now he looked strangely luminous, as daylight filtered into his workshop.

David, too, peered at the old man. Was there such a thing as the "essence" that made the light glow? Perhaps Miriam or Elizabeth knew. He would make it a point to ask them sometime.

But for now, time was passing with much to do. Through the window of the hut, Elizabeth could see the sun rising high in the eastern sky. The hour was getting late and the journey ahead of them was long.

They thanked the Lamplighter for his hospitality. Smiling, he filled their pouches with delights from his garden.

It was then that David saw a faraway look in the old man's face.

"Take this with you," the old man said, removing a small vessel of oil from one of his cabinets and tucking it into Elizabeth's hands. "It is a very thick blend that may come in handy."

"Thank you," Elizabeth said again.

Then David and Miriam shook the Lamplighter's hand, and they were on their way.

The Beggar

T WAS WRITTEN IN THE BOOK OF THE prophets that "whosoever shall be invited to Life's Feast must bring a Guest." David often pondered this inscription, which Joshua liked to quote. But the boy did not truly understand what it meant until he, Miriam, and Elizabeth met the Beggar Woman.

They had been walking all day and were almost to the top of the mountain pass, just above the Great Stone Quarry, when they saw her. By the side of the road, on a rock in the sun, she was seated alone, with a bowl in her hand. Old and wrinkled, with sunken cheeks and a furrowed brow, she wore a tattered tunic and a careworn smile. Each time someone walked by, she pleaded for mercy.

"Alms for the poor?" she called out. "Will you open your heart today and give alms to the poor?"

Hearing her, Miriam uncorked her water pouch and gave the Beggar Woman a refreshing drink. Then she escorted her to the shade of a nearby tree where Elizabeth set out figs, dates, olives, and other luscious treats from the Lamplighter's grove.

If you get invited to life's feast, bring a guest, David thought as he looked on.

Ravenous, the Beggar Woman ate like a wolf coming off lean times. The generous meal filled her empty stomach and brightened her smile. She was happy and content with what she had received.

But there were other delights in store.

Miriam reached into her sack and drew out a fresh garment to replace the Beggar Woman's torn tunic. Elizabeth washed and plaited her new friend's long white hair. And David rubbed herbs into the old woman's hands to soften the thick calluses that had come from living life as a wilderness dweller.

Like nurses, they tended to her as best they could. They addressed her needs until there were no needs left.

"How can I repay you?" the Beggar Woman asked when

they were finished. Her eyes were full of happiness. A tear ran down her cheek.

"You walk a rough road," Elizabeth said. "What led you to this place?"

"My tale is all I have," the woman said. "Shall I tell it?"

They nodded and listened as she told her story.

THE BEGGAR WOMAN'S STORY

IN THE VILLAGE OF MY FAMILY, AT THE HOUR OF MY BIRTH, A drought prevailed. The fields were parched. The crops had wilted. And the fish lay gasping on the banks of the streams.

"God is angry," the clerics told the people. "We must prescribe new laws."

But before the clerics acted, the skies opened up. Happy children danced in the rain. Old women caught freshwater in earthen jugs. And the midwife who had pulled me from my mother's loins reminded the people of the wise man who said, "A baby is God's promise that life must go on."

Was I?

My father was uneasy.

"This child wears a caul," he said, recoiling in fear. Only when the peculiar skin was cut from my head and buried behind the barn did he lay me at my mother's breast to drink from the fountain of love.

But the trouble was just beginning. When my father's cow went dry, he recorded my birth story in the Book of Suspicions. When locusts swarmed his field, he blamed me for the infestation and told my mother that the time had come to act.

Do not judge her. Do not scold her. Like a frightened donkey with a bit in her mouth, my mother did as she was told.

One day, when the market wagon came, she covered me in animal skin and slipped me in among the lambs and sheep bound for market. A merciful farmer would find me and take me home—I believe she held this hope in her heart.

But the farmers did not want me. The merchants would not keep me. The potters kept me at arm's length. I was black-marked, blacklisted, a black sheep, sent from place to place. The future looked grim and black.

One day, a shopkeeper gave me a begging bowl and took me to the mountain pass.

"Stay here," she said, "where the bushes are lush and the

streams are strong. I think you will find that many mammals walk here."

"What do you mean?" I asked.

"God's kingdom is divided," she said. "There are warm-
blooded animals who nurture and give. When they look,
they see. Where there is need, they provide. But there are
reptiles, too, with cold skin, hooded eyes, and small hearts."

Not understanding, I stood there alone, extending my
bowl. In time, the shopkeeper's words became clear to me.
Two kinds passed. One saw my suffering and tried as best
as they could to alleviate it. But others walked on, neither
caring nor bothering.

When I lay down at night, I asked Mother Nature to
instruct me.

"What shall I think?" I asked the wind and the stream
and the trees that counseled me often.

Love anyway, whispered the wind.

Be kind no matter what, the rustling trees told me.

Judge not lest you be judged, said the burbling brook.

"In time, I learned to find the good and praise it, lest cyni-
cism and sorrow thwart my soul."

"Thank you for telling your tale," Elizabeth said when the woman was finished. "Now we know you. One who tries to find the good."

When the Beggar Woman had finished her story, the hour was late. Elizabeth, Miriam, and David decided to bed down for the night in the small, dry cave the Beggar Woman called home.

There they all slept soundly, their stomachs full. For they had sat at table together, as host and as guest, and enjoyed the great feast.

Lessons for Elizabeth

HE NEXT MORNING, ELIZABETH ROSE early, picked berries, and set out a simple breakfast of fruits and nuts for the others. This was her way—to make sure that everyone had what was needed, that they were cared for and content.

Since her days as a small child growing up in the royal house, Elizabeth had always tried to be good and kind, following the example of her mother and grandmother before her. Both women were caregivers in the royal infirmary, tending the sick. Both had worked long years and met great challenges with fierce courage.

On one particular occasion, when Elizabeth was still very small, the King had declared war on a neighboring community and a bloody battle had ensued. Wounded and dying soldiers were flooding into the sick ward, where Elizabeth's grandmother and mother were in charge of relief efforts.

"We are stretched to the limits," an attendant told Elizabeth's grandmother. "How shall we serve?"

"Let us turn together, like spokes in a great wheel," she said. "Smooth and steady is the way."

The women listened and did as asked.

And the sick were tended.

And the wounded were healed.

And all that needed doing was done.

But afterward, when the day drew to a close, a great shroud of sorrow descended over the palace. Wives had lost husbands. Mothers had lost sons. Sisters had lost brothers. Children had lost fathers. A great hole had been gouged in the heart of the royal house as the dead were dressed for burial.

Elizabeth's grandmother saw to the fallen, dried the tears of the grief-stricken, then called all the women together. Her voice, normally strong, trembled as she spoke.

"Enough," she said. "Enough bloodshed and killing. Let each who has a heart arise and do what you can as mothers, wives, daughters, sisters, and aunts to stop the senselessness that takes from us our husbands, brothers, sons, uncles, and nephews. End the strife that kills and maims, and drink from the chalice of love."

That day, all returned to their quarters and cradled their young even more tenderly than before. In the air was the sentiment that she who wishes to move the world must move herself, that women harbored a great and mighty power to be the change they wished to see in the world.

But the next morning, Elizabeth's grandmother was called before the King's councillor.

"You arouse our servants with your 'Great Declaration of Enough,'" he said. "You defy our authority. A price must be paid."

The angry councillor confined Elizabeth's grandmother to the tapestry room. There she worked alone, repairing fabric, until her death. She was buried near the soldiers whose wounds she had treated that fateful day in the infirmary.

But her words lived on in many hearts. Elizabeth never forgot her grandmother's plea that each woman be an instrument of peace. That she who wishes to move the world must first move herself to action. That a great transformation would come when the sword was replaced with the chalice of love. Though she was young, Elizabeth vowed to spread those words as far and as wide as she could.

But for now, she had simpler goals—there was breakfast to serve. The sun was rising and everyone was ready to eat. The Beggar Woman, Miriam, and David had awakened and were sitting together and talking.

"Where are you going?" the Beggar Woman said.

"To find the Well That Never Runs Dry," Elizabeth replied. "I have dreamed of it."

"Many have gone looking for it," the Beggar Woman said. "But none has returned. Perhaps they did not know the secret of the sun and the clouds."

Elizabeth, Miriam, and David were quiet. They watched as the Beggar Woman tipped her head into the wind and listened as the gentle breeze spoke to her.

"You must enter the quarry when the sun is beginning to wane," she said. "Wait for the cloud cover—it will shield you from the last scorching rays of the late-afternoon sun. When the clouds come, it is time to move. Be quick. Do not delay. No one can survive in the Great Stone Quarry or the Sun Maze in the intense heat, when the sky is clear. Sun on stone is death."

Miriam, Elizabeth, and David thanked the Beggar Woman and asked her if she would come with them on their journey. They did not want to leave her alone in the wilderness. But she was old and her legs were tired and she was strangely content in her circumstance.

"I am with my mother," she said, leaning over and putting the palm of her hand on the ground. "And a mother is a gift."

"We will miss you," David said. Then he took her hand and asked her to tell another tale.

And so she told a tale that contained a warning.

⮰ THE HIGH HOLY HYPOCRITE ⮱

A FARMER ON THE MOUNTAIN PASS FELL DEATHLY ILL ONE day as he traveled to market.

"Help," he cried out in desperation. "If someone does not come quickly, I will perish."

Time passed. No one came. And so the man prepared to meet his maker. He was confessing his sins and seeking forgiveness when, out of nowhere, a Holy Man on a steed appeared. Dressed in pristine robes embroidered with gold threads, the man had large rings on his fingers and jewel-encrusted sandals on his feet. Even his saddle was adorned with precious stones.

"Brother," the Holy Man called out to the farmer on the ground beneath him. "I see you suffer. Your pain is great. But a crowd in the next village is waiting for my talk on the Higher Law. What will my followers think if I arrive late, in sullied robes?"

As the Holy Man sped off, the farmer sobbed, knowing that the last grains of sand were slipping through the hourglass of his life. Death was almost upon him when, out of nowhere, a Woman of Ill Repute appeared. Her face was smudged with dirt and her hair was disheveled. On her arms were angry lash marks inflicted by the clerics for her alleged misdeeds.

"Brother," she said, mopping the sick man's brow and giving him water. "I am here now. Keep faith."

The sick farmer flashed a weak smile, then closed his eyes as fever engulfed him. All the while, the woman held his hand, refusing to give up hope, though the farmer's illness was grave. Her mere presence was a force.

Then, as dusk fell, the man sat up, healthy, hungry, and restored.

"How can I repay you?" he asked the woman.

"Tell no one of your association with me," she said, "or

your name will be as black as the silt at the bottom of the riverbed."

"Woman," the farmer replied. "A Holy Man left me to die, yet you stopped to tend me. Who is greater—the one who touts the law yet places himself above it? Or the scorned one who comforts the sick?"

Humbled by the farmer's kind words, the Woman of Ill Repute said she was grateful. Then she went on her way.

The Beggar Woman ended her story, paused, and then tipped her head into the wind.

"Beware the one whose works betray their words," she said. "For actions speak louder."

They nodded, stroked the Beggar Woman's cheek as her father never did, and soon they resumed their journey.

The Great Stone Quarry

HEN THEY REACHED THE CREST, THEY saw it—the Great Stone Quarry. Set into the cliffs, the jagged outcropping of shiny white marble had given life to dwellings, walls, monuments, and temples until one fateful day when a mysterious flood swamped the quarry. That day, excavation was halted and the workers fled, never to return.

Now, consulting the tapestry, Elizabeth and Miriam were keen to forge ahead. The waters had long receded. The site was dry, stony, and still. A mystical calm coming out of the place pulled the women forward.

But David was sullen.

"Please, sister," the boy said. "I am hungry. Can you give me something to eat?"

Elizabeth told the boy that she had spotted a stream on a lower ridge. "Stay with the donkeys and do not wander," she said. "I will go to catch fish with Miriam and we will be back soon."

But as the boy sat, waiting, he heard heavy feet crushing small stones.

"Hello," called a Stranger who emerged from the mouth of a small, hidden cave. The man had a heavy pack on his back. He was sweaty from carrying a heavy load on such a sweltering hot day.

"I see you have two donkeys," the man continued. "What a burden. Two mouths to feed. Two animals to graze. Two in need of water. Has no one told you that the best things in life aren't things?"

Joshua had often counseled David about worldly possessions. The shepherd lived simply. So, too, did Elizabeth.

But the animals were not possessions. They were David's friends.

"They carry me when I am tired," the boy told the man. "They quell my fear when I am lonely. And they love me always, asking nothing in return."

"But who needs such excess?" the Stranger persisted. "Let me lighten your load. I will take one of these beasts off your hands and see that it gets to a needy family." As he spoke, the man bent over to pluck a few blades of grass. It seemed he wished to feed the donkeys.

But as he leaned forward, he lost his balance and tumbled to the ground, and his pack tipped over, spilling an assortment of urns, necklaces, rings, and trinkets. The Stranger who preached simplicity looked like a traveling market stall.

Beware the one whose works betray their words, David thought.

"Let me help you," David said as the man scrambled to gather up his goods. But in a rush to sling his pack back up on his shoulder, the Stranger bumped one of the donkeys, which reared up.

"Whoa!" the Stranger shouted, trying to calm the animal, generating a dust cloud like one David had never seen. The donkey was soon in a full-blown fit, braying and harrumphing uncontrollably.

"This animal is ill tempered," the Stranger shouted, stumbling around in a blind rage. "No trader will want it—you've wasted my time."

Pulling a sharp switch from his pack, the Stranger raised his arm in the air and was poised to strike David when Miriam and Elizabeth came up the path. Seeing the women caused the Stranger to drop the switch and escape on foot.

Elizabeth took David in her arms. She held him tightly as he spoke.

"My father punished me often," the boy said as memories flooded back of cruel beatings doled out for small infractions. Old trials haunted the boy. His scars were deep.

Miriam drew close, placing her hands on the boy's back.

"We will camp here tonight and make a fire," Elizabeth said. She picked up the Stranger's switch and told David that it would serve as kindling.

Then they all joined hands and said a prayer of thanks for tragedy averted.

From Hard to Soft

ON THE THIRD DAY OF THE JOURNEY, they descended the mountain pass and reached the edge of the Great Stone Quarry. Miriam sat down, rested her tired feet, and braided her hair. David gathered small stones to build a little wall. And Elizabeth lay down in a soft patch of grass to collect her thoughts.

It seemed like an eternity since they had left home, following Elizabeth's dream to find the Well That Never Runs Dry. The journey had led them to many memorable people, each with a message.

The Storyteller told them of each person's ability to create or destroy, according to the power of intention.

The Lamplighter told them it was not enough to light the fire—one must tend the flame to keep it bright.

The Beggar Woman spoke of the need to find the good and praise it, avoiding judgment, no matter what.

And the Stranger gave proof that actions speak louder than words.

It was while thinking these things that Elizabeth fell into a deep sleep. She dreamed she was in a faraway place with green grass and rolling hills. The Old Woman was there, sitting on her trunk, happy to see a visitor.

"So you are back," the Old Woman said. "And you have questions."

"How do you know?" Elizabeth said.

"By that look on your face. You've seen the little one cry out in pain. Old wounds run deep. The sadness is lasting."

"Yes," Elizabeth said. "What can I do?"

Elizabeth watched the Old Woman go into her trunk and retrieve a vessel of balm, which she rubbed into the tough, thick skin that had formed on her hands from long years of difficult work.

"The balm softens what is hard," the Old Woman said. "The balm heals. But the balm takes time." As she spoke, the Old Woman kept rubbing in a circular motion. Again and again, she dipped her fingers into the balm and applied it to the rough spots.

Elizabeth nodded, then reached out to feel the Old Woman's hands. The resin had already begun to work. The hands, somewhat softer, were also warm and pulsating.

"Keep heart," the Old Woman said. "Let your faith sustain you. Believe in the healing force."

"And if I do?" Elizabeth said.

But that was it. The dream was done.

David

AVID WAS GROWING. LIKE A YOUNG PLANT in the hot sun, he shot up in leaps and bounds, confident that one day he would be the tallest in the family.

"Soon I will be able to reach the sweetest fruit on the highest branches," he told Elizabeth one day. "Soon I will tower over Joshua." Elizabeth laughed at the good-natured boast. But she used the occasion to tutor the boy, saying, "Stand tall and reach high. But always remember that a mighty heart is the true measure of a man's stature."

David listened, knowing his sister always spoke the truth in love and loved the truth.

Since coming to live with Joshua and Elizabeth, David had begun studying with the Old Scribe in a nearby village.

The master was teaching the boy to make ink and dye from flowers; dry papyrus leaves; make scrolls; and, most of all, to cherish the Word.

"In the beginning was the Word and the Word was good," the Old Scribe often said. "Use words carefully."

The boy listened. The boy learned. But David's most powerful lessons always came while walking and talking with Joshua each day.

On one occasion, while out on the hill with the sheep, Joshua asked David how his studies were going.

"The Old Scribe is kind," David said. "The old teacher is generous, too. But the new apprentice, Isaac, is stingy. He borrows ink and papyrus from the others but never shares. 'Do not befriend Isaac,' I warn all newcomers. 'He is the stingy boy.'"

Joshua listened, mindful of Isaac's circumstances. The boy was the last of ten children born to poor and elderly parents. Perhaps Isaac had not had enough of the healing balm of love rubbed into his young soul.

"We will invite Isaac to walk with us one day so that you can get to know him better," Joshua said. "I think you will like him."

In the meantime, Joshua told David a teaching story drawn from folklore.

⚓ THE TALE OF CHICKEN FEATHERS ⚓

THERE ONCE WAS A BOY WHO SPOKE HARSHLY OF A FELLOW student, calling him lazy. The unflattering gossip circulated far and wide before it was discovered to be as unfair and untrue as it was unkind.

"How shall I make amends for my gossip?" the boy asked his mother. "I have maligned an innocent one with falsehoods."

"Pluck a chicken," the boy's mother said, catching her son off guard with the odd suggestion. "Put the feathers in a sack and go up on the mountaintop and release them. As each feather floats in the air, let it carry a prayer to heaven for the boy wounded by your words. When you have done as I have instructed, return to me."

The boy did as told. Then he returned to his mother.

"I have done as you asked," the boy said proudly. "I have climbed to the top of the mountain and released a sack of feathers. Each floated gently on the breeze. It was a most beautiful sight. As the feathers sailed, I asked heaven to bless the boy I wronged."

"Good," the boy's mother said. "Now, go and collect all the feathers that blew away. Gather them up and present them to the hurt boy, with your sincere apology."

When Joshua finished the story, David flashed a knowing smile. He then fetched a stylus and made a list on a small piece of parchment that he always carried around with him. On it he wrote:

> *Speak no evil.*
> *Be kind.*
> *Be brave.*
> *No matter what.*

Now, as he stood with Elizabeth and Miriam at the mouth of the Great Stone Quarry, the boy ran his finger over the little piece of parchment tucked in his pocket. Its wisdom could guide him in any situation—he was confident.

But now there was work to do.

Rolling out the small tapestry, Elizabeth and Miriam studied the picture symbols woven in red, gold, and blue

thread on the small white square of cloth. Where should
they begin?

There were eight icons arranged in a mysterious pattern.
There were icons for cliffs, a sun, walls, a cave, and a pool
as well as symbols for a little chest, a key, and some sort of
hole in the ground. If what the Lamplighter told them was
correct, there was a Sun Maze situated at the north end of
the Great Stone Quarry, with a pool just beyond the Sun
Maze inside some type of cave.

Beyond that, nothing was clear—except for the warning.

Elizabeth remembered the words of the Beggar Woman—
go when the sun is waning; sun on stone is death.

Rolling up the tapestry, Elizabeth reminded the others
of the need to wait. Then she led the way to the cool shade
of a tree on the edge of the quarry, where they sat.

It was the longest wait of her life.

A Time to Act

THE SUN WAS BEGINNING TO DIP IN THE western sky. A thick bank of clouds had suddenly rolled in. But there were still a few good hours of light left to work with. The time had come to act.

Linking hands, Elizabeth, Miriam, and David walked into the haunted stone yard. It was a mysterious canyon of scattered ruins where chisels, hammers, measuring sticks, mallets, old knives, saws, and picks lay strewn about, frozen in time, on top of giant slabs of white marble. Some of the implements were rusted—perhaps discarded by workers fleeing the aftermath of a torrential rain.

"This way," David said, encouraging the others to follow him along a well-worn path heading north. They had not gone far when they found themselves near a strange sequence of six-foot-high marble walls erected at odd angles. Why had such a large, labyrinthine structure been built at the back of a stone yard? Was this maze meant to shield a gathering spot where only a chosen few could enter? Who were they and where had they gone?

Elizabeth, Miriam, and David were confused but excited.

"Look! Miriam said, pointing to a pair of upright columns with a plinth across the top. The columns formed an entrance that was inscribed with the following:

> *Come Drink at My Well*
> *All Who Thirst*
> *And I Will Refresh You*

Elizabeth wanted to keep moving forward into the Sun Maze. She stepped through the columns. But Miriam was cautious.

"Wait!" she called out.

With Elizabeth and David looking on, the old seamstress bent over and began unraveling the hem of her light blue garment. Using one hand as a spool, she looped the blue thread around and around until she had a long length of string on her bony wrist. She would use the thread to

keep her beloved young cousin safe, to anchor her when she
entered the Sun Maze with a thin, cotton umbilical cord.

"Miriam," Elizabeth said, looking on. "You mystify me.
No friend is more resourceful."

But Miriam did not answer. Her mind was fixed on po-
tential pitfalls.

"You must carry a torch," she said, "and be on the look-
out for vipers—"

"Better still," David interrupted, "let me go in your place.
I can be quick."

Elizabeth was grateful for their offers. But this trial was hers.

"If there is danger to face," she said, "then I accept it.
But if I do not return"—she paused, choking on her words—
"tell Joshua of my undying love for him."

As she spoke the shepherd's name, a tear rolled down
her cheek. She wondered about the shepherd. Where was
he? Something told her that he was near. Was it possible?
Intuition said she would soon see him. She hoped and prayed
her senses were right.

But there was no time to delay. Now there was work to do.

She kissed David, hugged Miriam, took the end of the thread
that was attached to Miriam's hand, and entered the maze.

Slowly, steadily, inch by inch, she made her way forward, not knowing what to expect but adhering to a simple plan— no matter what, she would keep her hand on the left wall, turning left at each decision point.

Holding on to Miriam's thread, Elizabeth pushed forward into the large stone puzzle. A short way in, she saw dry, bleached bones that crackled underfoot, echoing the sounds of death and dread. Unnerved, she lost touch with the wall, became confused, and soon reached a dead end. So she returned to the entrance, where Miriam and the boy screamed in delight at the sight of her. Hugging her tightly, they did not want to let her go back into the Sun Maze.

But Elizabeth was keen to try again. Entering a second time, she decided to keep her hand on the right wall of the maze, always turning right each time there was a choice. As she moved forward, Miriam let out the string, giving Elizabeth as much slack as she needed.

And then, suddenly— Eureka! Elizabeth saw an exit from the maze leading to the mouth of an underground grotto. Tiny shafts of daylight filtered into the grotto from cracks in the rock ceiling above it. Air and light made seeing and breathing possible, so Elizabeth stepped forward toward a pool of water that was set into the ground and surrounded by nine white marble pillars. An inscription on a frieze in the wall above the pool said:

> *Let us baptize by water, not tears*
> *Let us pour cool water on the hot embers*
> *of affliction*

What did the inscription mean? Who congregated in this temple-like place?

Elizabeth pushed on, carefully inspecting the place and noticing an inscription on each of the pillars:

Mercy. Kindness. Patience. Love. Forgiveness. Justice. Gentleness. Generosity. Unity.

Unity.

Elizabeth wondered what "unity" had to do with the rest of the words. She briefly chewed on the idea, but there was more to see.

Beyond two of the pillars, set back from the pool, was a stone table illuminated by shafts of soft light filtering down through cracks in the rock ledge. This table held a small but intricately carved wooden ark. Her eyes widening, Elizabeth was eager to get to the ark. To open its door. *To know its mysteries.* Perhaps it would shed some light on the dream that had called her here.

But as she crept forward toward the ark and tried to open its door, she realized that she needed a key—another icon depicted in the tapestry. Circling behind the table, Elizabeth saw a bucket on a rope suspended into a hole in the ground—a small well—*just as the tapestry had indicated!* She pulled up the bucket and there it was—a tiny metal key!

Her thoughts were now racing. Would the key fit? What was in the ark?

Trembling, Elizabeth approached the ark and tried fitting the key into the lock. She jiggled the little key, delicately finessing the lock. But the lock was rusty—the key would not go in. She tried again and again. But she had no luck.

Stepping back, she tried another tactic—lifting the ark. If it was not too heavy, she would carry it out of the sanctuary, back through the Sun Maze, to the Great Stone Quarry. But the ark was somehow attached to the stone table and would not budge.

Elizabeth felt that fate had called her here. But fate would have to wait. The light was fading. Following the thread, she made her way back through the Sun Maze, into the arms of Miriam and David.

A Thick Coat of Oil

IKE WATER FROM A FALL, THE WORDS tumbled out of Elizabeth's mouth. Breathless and exuberant, she described what she had seen.

"Beyond the Sun Maze is a sacred grotto that encloses a pool, stone columns, and an ark," she said. "The ark is sealed shut by a rusty lock."

"Let me go," David said. "If the lock does not open, I can carry the ark."

"Stitching and mending have made me strong," Miriam said. "Let me go and do the work."

Elizabeth smiled. She was grateful for her family's support. But there had to be another solution.

It was then Elizabeth remembered the vial of oil the Lamplighter had given them. The oil was thick. Perhaps she could use it to loosen the lock.

"Woman," Miriam said, hearing Elizabeth's idea, "your plan is inspired."

But the plan would have to wait. Darkness had fallen. Finding a tree on the edge of the Great Stone Quarry, they bedded down to sleep for the night. At least for now, Elizabeth's quest would be deferred one more day.

The Dream

LIZABETH SLEPT. SHE DREAMED SHE WAS in a faraway place with green grass and rolling hills. At the crossroads of this mysterious place was the Old Woman with long silver hair, who was sitting on top of a trunk.

"Hello," the Old Woman said. "You're back and you have questions."

"How do you know?" Elizabeth asked.

"By that look on your face," the Old Woman said. "In a world full of dominators wielding the sword, you wonder what hope there is to baptize by water, not tears, and to cool the fire in the furnace of affliction. Hurt and heartache come in so many ways."

"This is the way of the world," Elizabeth said.

"But you seek a new way," the Old Woman said. "You told me so. You thirst for the Well That Never Runs Dry."

The Old Woman got up from her trunk and went to stand by a roaring fire at an outdoor hearth. The fire was hot and high, its embers red and glowing. The Old Woman was tormented by the flames. Her anguish was palpable.

"What shall I do?" the Old Woman said, trying to shield herself from the scorching heat. "Who will help me?"

Strangers passed by and scoffed at the circumstance. "You caused the fire," they told the Old Woman. "You are to blame. Now suffer."

But then, out of nowhere, helpers appeared to douse the flames.

"Who are you?" the Old Woman asked. But they were not self-seeking and did not answer. They simply worked until the task was completed.

Elizabeth watched the Old Woman tap on her chest.

"But I say to you that until there is a change of heart, until the Old Law is replaced by the New Law, until judgment is replaced by love, the furnace of affliction will rage out of control."

"Yes," said Elizabeth. "I understand."

The Lamplighter's Hut

OSHUA WAS TIRED. FOR SEVERAL DAYS, HE had been helping to resettle the victims of the flood on the High Ground. Carrying stones, laying foundations, and building new dwellings were strenuous tasks that had sapped his strength.

Now, eager to be home with David and Elizabeth, he had walked all night with his sheep, exhausting the oil in his lamp. When he realized that his supplies were depleted, he went by the Lamplighter's hut.

"Hello," the shepherd said. "I have walked all night and need oil for my lamp."

Surprised to see a customer before dawn, the Lamplighter got what the traveler needed from his supply cabinet.

"Where are you coming from?" the Lamplighter asked.

"I have been on the High Ground, resettling the victims of the flood," the shepherd said.

"You must be Joshua, the shepherd, are you not?" the Lamplighter asked. He looked more carefully into the traveler's round, friendly face, which was framed by wavy, shoulder-length brown hair.

"How do you know?" Joshua answered, smiling.

"Three travelers in search of the Well That Never Runs Dry have just passed through this village," the Lamplighter explained. "Elizabeth, who had dreamed of the well, was on the journey with her brother, David, and her cousin Miriam."

The Lamplighter showed Joshua the mysterious tapestry and described the geography of the Great Stone Quarry, where the travelers had gone to look for the well.

Joshua thanked the Lamplighter for his insights, then turned toward the mountain pass, saying, "I am on my way."

The Temptation of Joshua

 INDING ELIZABETH WAS ALL THAT MATTERED now. The Lamplighter had told Joshua of her journey with David and Miriam to the Great Stone Quarry. The trio had traveled over the steep mountain pass that was slow to walk with sheep. But Joshua was in a hurry. Was there a quicker way to go?

And then it dawned on him—he would take a shortcut through the Arid Region where the Python Woman lived with her Cult of Snake Worshippers. The Python Woman was an outcast who was said to use unnatural powers to lure unsuspecting travelers into her tribe. The elders excoriated her. The clerics condemned her. And many feared her.

But the shepherd was not afraid. His faith made him whole. His mighty heart would guide him. Besides, no obstacle on earth could keep him from getting to his family.

Leaving the Lamplighter's hut, the shepherd looked to

the rising sun and promised the dawn that he would keep his heart as light as a feather. Then he pulled up the hood of his tunic to shield him from the intense heat of the Arid Region and set off on his walk.

For a long time, the journey was uneventful. Joshua drove his sheep forward in the dry, flat, barren landscape, making sure they all kept pace. Abba and Babba, Lev and Zev, Jonah and Iona, Little and Fiddle—each member of the flock was safe and accounted for.

But then, suddenly, Joshua heard a voice.

"Here," a woman called out. "Come close. Do not be afraid. I won't hurt you."

She was seated on the ground, behind a bush beneath a canopy, with a group of acolytes at her feet. The Python Woman's followers had a vacant stare in their eyes as they fanned their leader, whose pale limbs poked out of the sleeves of a strange black tunic.

"Come see my snakes," she said to Joshua. "Feast your eyes on me. Do not be afraid." As she spoke, a bunch of snakes threaded through her hair and coiled around her limbs and neck. When one of the larger creatures began to choke her, the Python Woman let out an ecstatic cry that delighted her acolytes, who fanned her even faster.

"Come closer, see for yourself," the Python Woman implored Joshua after the snake had loosened its grip. The acolytes cleared a path so that the shepherd could approach.

But Joshua was circumspect. Cold, clammy snakes held no appeal for him. He much preferred warm-blooded animals. Sheep, goats—all mammals, really. He was also concerned about time—there was none to waste. He needed to keep moving and get to his family.

And yet something in the Python Woman—was it her soft, alluring voice? her penetrating eyes?—was exerting a strong pull over him. Joshua was starting to weaken. *What harm was there in taking a quick look?* he thought. The woman's eyes were beckoning him. And the slithering of the snakes was beginning to mesmerize him.

He had begun to move toward the Python Woman when a voice inside him whispered, *Elizabeth. David. Miriam.* In the stillness of his soul, he could hear the soft murmuring of those names, again and again.

"I am in a hurry," Joshua said to the Python Woman, snapping to attention.

Elizabeth. David. Miriam. The names repeated in his head.

The Python Woman flashed an angry look that was quickly replaced with a strange grin. Joshua had never seen such an unnatural, frozen mask before. The Python Woman's smile did not reach her eyes.

"Where are you going?" the Python Woman asked.

"To find the Well That Never Runs Dry," Joshua answered.

"Pity," said the Python Woman. "Because it doesn't exist. Many have gone looking for it. But none has returned. Perhaps they get lost in the Sun Maze. It's a dangerous place that can burn human flesh to a blackened crisp."

Joshua's heart began to beat rapidly. The thought of his family in trouble was more than he could bear.

Keep your heart as light as a feather, he thought, trying to stay in control of himself.

"I must go now," Joshua said. "I need to find Elizabeth."

"Elizabeth?" the Python Woman said. "Can she charm snakes as I do? My creatures strangle me with affection. Come closer. See for yourself."

Glancing at the snakes, Joshua again began to weaken. Their sinuous movements, coupled with the woman's alluring voice, were pulling him off center. He was no longer in command of himself. No longer captain of his soul. The power of free will was draining out of him.

And then the unthinkable happened. Just as Joshua's knees began to buckle, a snake escaped from the Python Woman's hair, slithered across the ground, and coiled around the leg of one of Joshua's sheep. The frightened animal began to squirm and bleat in a frantic way that flustered the entire flock, which began racing around and around in sympathetic circles. Chaos soon reigned.

"Look what you've done!" the Python Woman shouted in a sharp tone that jolted Joshua from his trance. Lunging forward, he yanked the snake off the sheep's leg and threw it into the distance, where it smashed against a rock. The acolytes began to wail, uncertain what the Python Woman would do next.

"Silence!" the mistress of snakes commanded. But she was no longer in charge of the scene. Now in command was Joshua, who had risen up. His staff held high, he addressed the acolytes, who were cowering by the Python Woman's feet.

"Can the crooked be made straight?" he asked. "Can the blind lead the blind? Yet your mistress walks in darkness."

A great silence fell over the place as Joshua kneeled down to comb his sheep, making sure they were free of vipers, nettles, burrs, and bristles. When he had determined that all of his animals were safe, he rose back up to his feet.

But the seduction was not over.

"Eat and drink with us," the Python Woman pleaded. "I promise a meal you will never forget." She held out a vessel marked with the emblem of snakes. But Joshua rebuked her, saying, "Man does not live by bread alone."

"My riches can fill a kingdom," the Python Woman said. "Let me show you my treasures." She pointed to a chest with golden trim that stood nearby.

"What would I profit," Joshua said, "if you gave all your riches to me but possessed my soul?"

And then, suddenly, the Python Woman's veneer of kindness fell away and was replaced by her naked ambition and lust for glory.

"Bow down and say my name and see what treasures you might behold," the Python Woman said. "Join my kingdom. Worship me."

But Joshua was no longer listening. Her spell broken, he had turned away. So, too, had the acolytes, who gathered up their things and began to return to the places from where they had come.

As for Joshua, he counted up his sheep and was soon again on his way, in search of his family.

Like the Lilies of the Field

IRST CAME SYLLABLES:

> "Ba-by
> Bas-ket
> Wa-ter
> Ma-ma"

Then sentences:

"You are the baby, in the basket, by the water, with his mama."

As the woman spoke, the baby's eyes seemed to twinkle back at her, saying, "And I am with my mother. What could be more perfect?"

Joshua stood back, hidden from view by the tall grass. It was midday. He had just come out of the Arid Region and was at the stream, looking for a place to water his sheep, when the peculiar language lesson came wafting through the air.

Ba-by. Bas-ket. Wa-ter Ma-ma.

Spoken carefully, patiently, from a bottomless well of gentleness that could never run dry, this was the language of mother love.

"Hello," the shepherd said, finally stepping forward and introducing himself. "I am Joshua and my sheep need water. I hope we are not a bother to you." As he spoke, his animals barged forward and dunked their faces into the stream.

At first cautious, the woman did not answer. Instead, she shielded her baby from the unfamiliar man until she saw the shepherd's warm, friendly face, knew he was gentle, and let down her guard.

"I am Martha," she said, introducing herself. "My baby is Joseph."

Though shy, the woman exchanged pleasantries, saying she lived in the nearby village with her husband, who worked for the Wagon Master. The noonday sun sat high overhead as the woman spoke, and she realized that it would soon be time to serve her husband's midday meal before the start of the caravan. Excusing herself, she prepared to leave.

At least for the moment, all seemed well.

But in an instant, everything changed. As she settled the baby in the basket, the infant's face became beet red and he began to cry inconsolably, drawing his feet up to his body in a fit of pain.

Alarmed, Joshua dropped his staff and approached the young mother, whose baby was now screaming and crying without halt.

"Woman," the shepherd said. "What must I do?" He offered to go for the physician in the village. But he did not know the house.

"Woman," he repeated. "What do you want from me?"

Calm, her attention on the baby, she picked up the child and put him firmly on her shoulder, both hands upon his back. The angry redness of the baby's face began to lessen as she rocked and swayed. His little arms and legs soon became unclenched. Shortly after, she placed him back in his basket, where he fell asleep.

Mystified, Joshua asked the young woman what she had done to relieve the child's pain.

"I did as the midwife instructed," the woman said. "The first time the baby stiffened, I brought him to the physician, who said there was no cure. But the midwife differed, saying, 'Let time have time. This, too, shall pass. Remember the lilies of the field,' she said. 'They toil not, neither do

they spin. For even Solomon in all his glory is not arrayed like one of these.'"

"And you were calm?" Joshua asked. "Like the lilies?"

But the young mother did not answer—her attention was on the child. Even as he slept, she soothed and stroked him with her gentle hands.

A short time later, when she was ready to return to the village, Joshua walked beside the woman, who held the basket in her hand and the baby on her shoulder.

"Where are you going?" she asked the shepherd.

"To find the Well That Never Runs Dry," Joshua said.

"They say it is only a short distance from here, near the Great Stone Quarry," the woman said. "The Wagon Master is about to go that way. Let him carry you and your sheep and you will arrive there quickly."

Happy to save time, Joshua thanked the woman, who gave him food for his journey and watched him board the wagon with his sheep. When the woman and her baby had departed, Joshua curled up among his animals and soon drifted off into a peaceful reverie.

On the Road Less Traveled

JOSHUA SLEPT.

He dreamed he was in a faraway place with green grass and rolling hills. At the crossroads of this mysterious place was an Old Man sitting on a trunk.

"Hello," said the Old Man. "Are you looking for something?"

"How do you know?" Joshua said.

"By that look on your face. Most people who come here are trying to find the Well That Never Runs Dry. I can point you to it. But I think you know the way. Take the road less traveled. Go with wise women who own the power. And honor the hands that heal."

"And if I do?" asked Joshua.

But that was it. The dream was done.

Back into the Breach

oshua! Where are you? I need you!

In the canyons of her mind, Elizabeth called out his name, certain he was near—her senses told her so. But would he come in time to join her quest? Dusk was beginning to fall, and she would soon return to the ark.

She was packing the vial of oil, ready to embark, when the sound of feet crushing stone echoed through the quarry.

"What was that?" David called out. Miriam became still. Elizabeth stopped in her tracks. They all looked around.

Suddenly, two sheep came ambling through the canyon. Sniffing David, they began to lick the boy as if he was a block of salt.

"Little! Fiddle!" David called out. He was about to get down on his knees to kiss them both when he saw Joshua coming up with the rest of his flock.

"Joshua!" they all cried out. "You are here! You have come!"

The shepherd kissed Elizabeth, hugged David, and was introduced to Miriam. Their joyful reunion was mixed with tears as he told her of his harrowing encounter with the Python Woman and of his meeting the young mother whose sick baby was restored to health.

For a few minutes, they all stood still, happy to be in the loving presence of one another.

But there was no time to linger. Dusk was falling, a bank of clouds rolled in, and Elizabeth was ready to move. She explained her purpose to Joshua, took him by the hand, and led him back through the Sun Maze, to the grotto.

"How far?" Joshua said, following Elizabeth's lead.

But she had no words, only resolve, as she moved ahead quickly, wishing to waste no time. She was two paces ahead of him, her right hand on the wall of the maze as she prepared for her meeting with destiny.

When they reached the mouth of the grotto, they paused and said a prayer of protection. Joshua took Elizabeth's hand, and together they entered the stillness of the sanctuary, where the shepherd beheld the pool, the ancient inscriptions, and the pillars. Elizabeth stood at the shepherd's side, remaining quiet as he took in the scene. Only time would tell if their plan would succeed.

Then, slowly, carefully, they approached the ark, where Elizabeth picked up the key, which lay on the table. She took the vial of oil from her side pouch and spread a thick coat of oil over the key, then slipped the implement into the lock. She turned the key to the left and gently tried to move the clasp. But it did not open.

"Be patient," Joshua said, believing that she could not be otherwise. Her elegant hands were always slow and loving when she brought new life into the world. He was always at her side then, whenever she needed him, to assist her in her work. This time was no different.

Elizabeth coated the key again, spreading a new layer of the oil over it. Then, oddly, she began to tremble. The impact of the moment was beginning to overwhelm her.

"Let me steady you," Joshua said, putting his hand on top of hers. He held and soothed her. Together they worked. And together they guided the key into the tumbler, turning it to the right, slowly, carefully. And then—suddenly—*click!* She was in.

"Please, God," Elizabeth prayed. "Guide me."

Elizabeth's hands grew steadier as the doors opened to reveal what appeared to be two marble tablets composing a book held together by a metal hinge.

"Open me!" this stone book seemed to cry out.

But time was of the essence. Elizabeth and Joshua wanted to get back to David and Miriam before darkness fell. There was still the maze to navigate.

After handing the tablets to Joshua, Elizabeth watched the shepherd secure them in his pouch. Reversing course, they then moved quickly, out of the grotto and into the maze.

For a short while, all seemed well.

But suddenly, Joshua stepped on a bone and twisted his ankle.

"Elizabeth," Joshua cried. "I am hurt!"

Alarmed, Elizabeth took Joshua's arm and escorted him back to the grotto, where he removed his sandal and dipped his foot into the cool water of the pool. Elizabeth put her hand on top of his shoulders, asking heaven to let the Oil of Serenity fill their lamps, keep them calm, and give them healing.

Meanwhile, back in the Great Stone Quarry, David and Miriam were beginning to worry. Where were Elizabeth and Joshua? Why had they not come back yet? It was getting late—night was beginning to fall. With it came danger. David could smell it, taste it, feel it.

"Shall I go for them?" David said.

"You are a boy, young and innocent," Miriam declared.

"If Elizabeth and Joshua need me," David asserted. "Then today I am a man." He lit his torch and, hugging the right wall, headed into the maze. Miriam kept watch over the sheep and the donkeys as he slipped into darkness.

Into the Valley of Death

ELLO-O-ELLO-ELLO."

David's voice bounced off the stone walls of the Sun Maze as he walked along, calling out into the night. Every so often, he would look up at the vast canopy of twinkling stars and marvel at the universe.

"The Great Plan is far more complex than you can ever know," Joshua once said, quoting the ancients. "God is too big and His plan too great for us to understand. Where were we when God put the stars in the sky and created the oceans? We are much too puny to comprehend."

David felt the enormity of these words as fear gripped him. He was alone, walking at night, in a maze that felt like a valley of darkness and death. The dry bones crunched beneath his feet. A bat flew overhead, mussing his hair and sending a chill up his spine. A snake slithered across the path in front of him and he flinched at the reptile's cold, clammy touch. A strange nocturnal animal—was it a possum?—flashed him a sinister glance from a corner of the maze. Like David, the animal seemed not to know where he was headed.

But David needed to stand tall. He needed to be a man. Joshua and Elizabeth were counting on him.

"Hello-ello-ello," he called out again. And then, miraculously, the sound came back.

"We are here," Joshua said. "In this grotto. Keep coming."

David held out his lantern, and Joshua and Elizabeth stepped out into the light. Banding together under the twinkling stars, David and Elizabeth let the shepherd lean on them. Then they made their way back out to Miriam, who was snuggled up with the sheep, beside the donkeys. Soon they were all huddled together, fast asleep.

The Morning After

HE SUN HAD RISEN. THE GRASS WAS SOFT. They lay on top of it in a row—all four of them—looking up at the vast blue sky and vividly recalling the harrowing adventure of the night before.

"Though I walked in a dark maze, I feared no evil, for you were by my side with your torch," Joshua said to the boy.

David smiled. He was happy to have been a shepherd to the shepherd, leading Joshua and Elizabeth to safety. The shepherd's ankle was better. The sheep were all accounted for—Abba and Babba, Jonah and Iona, Little and Fiddle, Lev and Zev. All were safe and sound.

But now they were eager to see what Elizabeth had found in the ark. Fetching his pouch, Joshua removed the stone book and laid it out on a small square of yellow cloth Miriam had placed on the ground. Joshua, Elizabeth, Miriam, and David all gathered around for their first close look.

The tablets were small—about six inches wide, eight inches high, and half an inch deep. Made of white marble, they were held together by a beautifully crafted metal hinge that glistened in the sun. The hand of an artisan was apparent in its fine filigree. A master had been at work.

Passing her hand over the smooth stone, Elizabeth felt the spot where someone had carved the initials "SMH."

"What does this mean?" Miriam asked, pointing to the letters.

From her time at the royal house, Elizabeth knew these letters were shorthand for the "Sisterhood of Midwives and Healers." This ancient, esoteric society of women was made up of freethinkers and intuitives who had been banished from the villages to the outlying mountain region for promoting the idea that women possessed the gift of healing in their hands.

"The Sisterhood said that healing was every woman's birthright," Elizabeth said. "They thought that women brought the powerful healing force of 'Mother Love' into the world and if enough women dared to 'own it,' a great time of health, healing, and harmony would come."

Mother Love. It was a simple idea. That was what made it so potent. Who had not held sick children to make them feel better? To hug and to hold were natural, God-given talents at every woman's fingertips.

But the men in power were afraid. Watching women flock to the Sisterhood to learn about healing touch led the clerics to limit who could treat the sick. Men were elevated while women were banned from all medical practice except "women's work," such as midwifery.

Defiant, the Sisterhood went underground and began to meet secretly, in caves and grottos, where sacred pools and still waters were used to help the sick achieve equilibrium of mind, body, and spirit. Miraculous stories were soon circulating about the lame who came to walk and the blind who came to see.

"The results were powerful," Elizabeth said. "And the powerful feared the results."

"Did the Sisterhood usurp authority?" Miriam asked.

"Quite the opposite," Elizabeth said. "They sought a society in which all could contribute their God-given talents. Everyone working together. Not domination but unity."

Unity. The inscription on one of the pillars floated back into Elizabeth's mind. Now she was pulled back to the task at hand—examining the tablets.

Spreading open the stones, Elizabeth read the first inscription:

> *Let all who have hearts arise and*
> *Drink from the Chalice of Love*

Shaken, Elizabeth remembered that her grandmother had spoken similar words many years earlier to comfort the women of the palace after a great battle had claimed many lives.

How did her grandmother know these words? Was she connected by ancestry with the Sisterhood? Her grandmother's cousin—Miriam's grandmother—had owned the tapestry that had led them to the Great Stone Quarry, the Sun Maze, the grotto, the sacred pool, and the ark. It was all in the family.

Baffled, Elizabeth looked at Joshua, Miriam, and David, who were at her side. Then she read the inscription on the second stone:

CREDO OF THE SISTERHOOD

*If I speak in the tongues of mortals
and of angels, but do not have love,
I am a noisy gong or a clanging cymbal.*

*And if I have prophetic powers, and
understand all mysteries and all knowledge,*

*And if I have all faith, so as to remove mountains,
but do not have love, I am nothing.*

*If I give away all my possessions,
and if I hand over my body so that I may boast,
but do not have love, I gain nothing.*

Love is patient;

Love is kind;

*Love is not envious or boastful or arrogant
or rude.*

It does not insist on its own way;

It is not irritable or resentful;

*It does not rejoice in wrongdoing, but rejoices in
the truth.*

It bears all things, believes all things,
hopes all things, endures all things.
Love never ends.
But as for prophecies, they will come to an end;
As for tongues, they will cease;
As for knowledge, it will come to an end.
For we know only in part, and we prophesy only
in part;
But when the complete comes, the partial will come
to an end.
But then we will see face to face.
Now I know only in part; then I will know fully,
even as I have been fully known.
And now faith, hope, and love abide,
These three;
And the greatest of these is love.

1 CORINTHIANS 13:1—13

The Well That Never Runs Dry

 O THERE IT WAS—THE SECRET REVEALED.
The well of love. The well that could be
found inside the human heart. The well
of kindness and goodness. Of generosity and patience.

Elizabeth had long been searching for this knowledge.
But had she not known it all along?

During her days growing up in the palace, she had been
taught by her mother and grandmother to love and be kind.
Both women were powerful vessels of goodness who used
their gentle hands and giving hearts to tend the sick and
comfort the grieving. And always, when Elizabeth was small,
they taught her to bless those who cursed her. To pray for
those who were hurtful. To love her enemies.

Some confused their gentleness with weakness. But they did not mind. They believed love was a softening agent that could melt hard hearts, and they risked themselves to prove it was true.

The royal midwife had also tutored Elizabeth in the nature of love, reminding her that love is not a reward bestowed on the deserving but a reward in itself.

Last but not least was Joshua, who raised her up with love and revealed its abiding strength.

Now, reflecting on the tablets, Elizabeth wondered what had happened to the Sisterhood. Driven to clandestine retreats in caves and grottos in the mountains, they had simply vanished—disappeared. Perhaps they were wiped out when the stone quarry was flooded. One might never know.

But the tablets had survived. The Credo—their manifesto—was intact. The same stonecutters who had built the Sun Maze to protect the Sisterhood from the oppressive authorities must have chiseled the tablets for the women who believed that love was the essence. The words of the Credo needed to be preserved for all time.

But what should happen next?

Elizabeth was not sure. The Storyteller had spoken of the coming "gentle time." The Sisterhood had spoken of women rising up, owning their power, and becoming partners in a new era of love. The Old Woman in the dream spoke of the world needing a change of heart. But what would it take to bring it about?

What would prompt more self-appointed helpers—earth angels, angels in the making—to come forward to pour cool water into the furnace of affliction and make the burning coals die down? It might require a Great Convocation. A *gathering*.

Elizabeth was lost in thought when Joshua's voice pricked her consciousness.

"We must spread this message far and wide," he said. "Let the word go out to all that 'Blessed are the peacemakers and healers.'"

"Yes," Miriam said. "I will embroider that message in my tapestries from this day forward."

"I will tell the tale of the Well That Never Runs Dry to all I know," David added. "Someday I will write the story down."

United in spirit and in purpose, they gathered up the sheep and the donkeys and began the long journey home.

The Journey Back

OME. THEY HAD BEEN AWAY FOR SO LONG that the place had become a distant memory, an abstract idea. Now finally, they were going back to the things they knew and loved.

"I will fill a bowl with figs and eat until I can eat no more," David said.

"I will sleep in the meadow, beneath the stars, until the cows come home," Joshua said.

"I will sit and sew until our tattered tunics are mended," Miriam said.

As for Elizabeth, she wished to call women together in a Great Convocation about love and healing.

Heading home, they met them all—the Beggar Woman, the Lamplighter, the Storyteller, and the deaf woman whose child had been washed away in the flood.

Drawing pictures on the ground, the deaf woman told Elizabeth that she had been sent to live in a community of castaways. With her hands, she spoke of the pain and sorrow of losing her child. With her hands, she let Elizabeth know that her reason for living was the orphaned children of the castaways. Caring for these children was a balm that made the woman feel less broken.

Did this woman deserve to suffer?

Had she brought this affliction upon herself?

Was she marked with a curse?

No. No. No. Full of kindness and love, this woman had done no wrong.

Why, then, was she afflicted by tragedy?

Why did bad things happen to good people?

Elizabeth could think only of the Credo—

For we know only in part . . .

God's plan was intricate and inscrutable. It was full of mystery.

Yet partial knowledge had not stopped the clerics, elders, and authorities from judging, blaming, and punishing.

Filled with a desire to dominate and control, their culture of blame was as corrosive as rust on metal. Only the Oil of Serenity could ease it.

Love was the answer. Love was the new imperative. If pain was a teacher, then love was the lesson.

Elizabeth knew this with every ounce of her being.

Build on Stone, Not Sand

S THEY NEARED HOME, THEY PASSED DAVID'S teacher, the Old Scribe.

"We must copy the Credo and circulate it far and wide," the Old Scribe said.

"Yes," said David. "I will ask my friend Isaac to help us."

"You must," Joshua said.

Reaching home, they made plans to build a scriptorium where they would store the tablets and provide a place for David to study and write. A sewing room would also be built for Miriam, who had agreed to live with them.

"Let us build on stone, not sand," the shepherd said. "Our foundation will always be one of love."

"Yes," Elizabeth said. "That which we value can never be taken from us."

As they broke through a wall into a room where Elizabeth's grandfather once stored some of his wife's belongings, they found a hidden recess. In it was a chest containing a tapestry embroidered with the following words:

Let All Who Have Hearts Arise—
And Own the Power

"Where did this come from?" Elizabeth asked. Miriam ran her fingers over the tapestry, which was artfully stitched with the illustration of a woman holding a chalice in her outstretched hand. By her foot, which was planted on a rock, was an unsheathed sword.

"It is a mystery," Joshua said. "We may never know."

And for now, they were too busy to find out. Hanging the tapestry on the wall of their dwelling, they began the task of making the old place new.

The Credo

F I SPEAK IN THE TONGUES OF MORTALS
and of angels, but do not have love, I am
a noisy gong or a clanging cymbal.

And if I have prophetic powers, and
understand all mysteries and all knowledge,

And if I have all faith, so as to remove mountains, but
do not have love, I am nothing.

If I give away all my possessions, and if I hand over
my body so that I may boast, but do not have love, I gain
nothing.

Love is patient;

Love is kind;

Love is not envious or boastful or arrogant or rude.

It does not insist on its own way;

It is not irritable or resentful;

It does not rejoice in wrongdoing, but rejoices in the truth.

It bears all things, believes all things, hopes all things, endures all things.

Love never ends.

But as for prophecies, they will come to an end;

As for tongues, they will cease;

As for knowledge, it will come to an end.

For we know only in part, and we prophesy only in part;

But when the complete comes, the partial will come to an end.

But then we will see face to face.

Now I know only in part; then I will know fully, even as I have been fully known.

And now faith, hope, and love abide,

These three;

And the greatest of these is love.

1 CORINTHIANS 13:1–13

A Word About the Credo

DRAWN FROM THE FIRST LETTER TO THE CORINTHIANS, THE
Credo is one of the most inspiring, beloved, and profound
passages of all time. Included in wedding ceremonies, eulo-
gies, and poetry collections, it describes the means to trans-
form our world.

Do you believe it?

Then take the Credo to heart. Don't keep your love
under a bushel. Right this minute—today—let the light of
your love shine for all to see!

Resources

Riane Eisler, author of *The Chalice and the Blade: Our History, Our Future*, who differentiates the dominator and partnership models

The New Oxford Annotated Bible: The New Revised Standard Version

> Luke 6:32–38, which is the basis of the Midwife's explanation of "What is love?"
>
> I Corinthians 13:1–13, for the Credo of the Sisterhood
>
> John 1:1–2, which gives rise to the Old Scribe's sentiment that "In the beginning was the Word"
>
> Job 8:11 for the question "Can the scribe's papyrus grow where there is no marsh?"
>
> Job 38, from which is drawn Joshua's comments to David, "Where were we when God put the stars in the sky . . ."

The Bible: The King James Version (World's Classics)

> Isaiah 48:10, for the phrase "The furnace of affliction"
>
> Matthew 16:26, the source of the remark "What would I profit if you gave all your riches to me but possessed my soul?"

Kent M. Keith, author of *Anyway: The Paradoxical Commandments*, who informs the author's belief to "Love anyway"

Carl Sandberg, for the line "A baby is God's promise that life must go on," quoted in the Beggar Woman's story

The phrase "Declaration of Enough," which may have originated in the simplicity movement and is adapted here for the author's purposes

"The Tale of Chicken Feathers" is the author's own version of a Hasidic tale offering a caution to guard your tongues— *lashon hara*—because words can harm

Witches, Midwives, and Nurses: A History of Women Healers by Barbara Ehrenreich and Deirdre English, for the historical perspective on women and medicine

Julia Ward Howe, for her "Mother's Day Proclamation," which informs the "Declaration of Enough" speech, spoken by Elizabeth's grandmother; the idea that we must baptize by water, not tears; and the idea that all who have hearts must arise

Here is the original "Mother's Day Proclamation," 1870, by Julia Ward Howe, author of *Reminiscences.*

Arise then . . . women of this day!

Arise, all women who have hearts!

Whether your baptism be of water or of tears!

Say firmly:

"We will not have questions answered by irrelevant agencies,

Our husbands will not come to us, reeking with carnage,

For caresses and applause.

Our sons shall not be taken from us to unlearn

All that we have been able to teach them of charity, mercy and patience.

We, the women of one country,

Will be too tender of those of another country

To allow our sons to be trained to injure theirs."

From the bosom of a devastated Earth a voice goes up with

Our own. It says: "Disarm! Disarm!

The sword of murder is not the balance of justice."

Blood does not wipe out dishonor,

Nor violence indicate possession.

As men have often forsaken the plough and the anvil

At the summons of war,

Let women now leave all that may be left of home

For a great and earnest day of counsel.

Let them meet first, as women, to bewail and commemorate the dead.

Let them solemnly take counsel with each other as to the means

Whereby the great human family can live in peace. . .

Each bearing after his own time the sacred impress, not of Caesar,

But of God—

If you enjoyed this book, you might also love
The Book of the Shepherd.

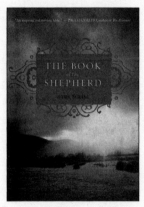

Available wherever books are sold